There And Back Again: About The Map of The Hobbit

by

Brian Sibley

HarperCollins*Publishers*

The author gratefully acknowledges the assistance of Richard G. Parlour in the compiling and checking of the text.

HarperCollinsPublishers
77–85 Fulham Palace Road
Hammersmith, London W6 8JB

First published in Great Britain by HarperCollins*Publishers* 1995
9 8 7 6 5 4

A catalogue record for this book is
available from the British Library

ISBN 0 261 10326 1

Printed in Great Britain

THE TITLE OF J. R. R. Tolkien's book *The Hobbit* tells you exactly *who* it is about, and the subtitle – 'There and Back Again' – tells you, right from the beginning, that it is going to be the story of a journey. That journey turns out to be a long, thrilling and highly dangerous one, during which the hobbit, Bilbo Baggins, encounters dwarves, elves, goblins, trolls, wild wolves, giant spiders and a fearsome fire-breathing dragon. All in all, the kind of exploit which ought never to have been undertaken without a map, which probably explains why, long before Tolkien had finished writing an account of Mr Baggins' journey, he was already drawing a map of it.

The story behind that map and that journey began some time in the early 1930s when J. R. R. Tolkien, Professor of Anglo-Saxon at Oxford University, was marking examination papers. Suddenly, out of nowhere, some words came into his head. At the time, he didn't know what they meant, but he scrawled them down on a sheet of paper which one of the examination candidates had left blank. 'In a hole in the ground,' he wrote, 'there lived a hobbit. . . '

Although it was a while before Tolkien had time to think about who that hobbit was and what he was going to do with him, an adventure eventually began to unfold in his mind and was written down. In what was to become the book's first chapter, 'An Unexpected Party', the author introduced Mr

Bilbo Baggins, a very well-to-do hobbit who lived at Bag-End, a comfortable hobbit-hole on The Hill, in the Shire.

Hobbits, said Tolkien, 'are (or were) a little people, about half our height', inclined to be fat in the stomach, with no beards (unlike dwarves) but lots of curly brown hair that grew not only on their heads but on the tops of their feet as well, which meant that (since they also had leathery soles) they rarely wore shoes. Hobbits dressed in bright colours, had clever brown fingers, good-natured faces and 'deep fruity laughs (especially after dinner, which they have twice a day when they can get it)'.

Nothing would normally have induced Bilbo Baggins – or any other hobbit – to go in search of so disturbing and uncomfortable a thing as an adventure; but it soon became clear that an adventure had finally come in search of him, because through his round front door marched thirteen dwarves and a wizard named Bladorthin.

For those who have read *The Hobbit* and do not remember a wizard named 'Bladorthin', it should be explained that Tolkien later decided to call this character 'Gandalf' – a name he had originally given to the chief dwarf, whom he then named 'Thorin'.

Gandalf was a curious old man with a long white beard, who wore a tall pointed blue hat, a grey cloak and a silver scarf. Bilbo remembered him as a wandering wizard who used to visit the Shire, telling wonderful tales about dragons, goblins, giants and the like, and bringing remarkable fireworks and extraordinary gifts – such as 'a pair of magic diamond studs that fastened themselves and never came undone till ordered'. What Bilbo (and probably Tolkien) had yet to discover was that Gandalf was a truly mighty magician.

As for the dwarves, they turned out to be surprising guests. First to arrive was Dwalin who had a blue beard tucked into a golden belt; next was Balin, an old-looking dwarf with a white beard; then came Kili and Fili with silver belts and yellow beards, followed by Dori, Nori, Ori, Oin and Gloin, Bifur, Bofur and Bombur who was 'immensely fat and heavy'. Last, but by no means least, was 'an enormously important dwarf', the great Thorin Oakenshield. Thorin's sky-blue hood with a silver tassel was soon hanging up in Bilbo's hall alongside two blue, two purple and two yellow hoods and others of dark-green, pale green, scarlet, grey, brown and white.

After the dwarves had eaten Bilbo out of house and home, they entertained the hobbit with stories and songs about their ancient people who, long years before, had worked as smiths. Deep underground, in hollow halls, hammer rang on anvil as the dwarves shaped and wrought their precious metals, carving goblets and harps of gold, forging swords with gem-encrusted hilts, making silver necklaces strung with flowering stars and crowns hung with dragon-fire.

Eventually, Bilbo discovered the real reason for this unexpected party. Thorin and his twelve companions were planning to set out on a long journey – across rivers and mountains,

through woods and forests – to the Lonely Mountain, far away in the east, in the hope of recovering the treasures of their ancestors which had been stolen, and were now being guarded, by the terrible dragon Smaug (or, as Tolkien first called him, Pryftan). Accompanying themselves on harp, flute and drum, the dwarves sang of the journey they had to take:

Far over the misty mountains cold
To dungeons deep and caverns old
We must away, ere break of day,
To claim our long-forgotten gold.

As Bilbo listened to the dwarf music, he felt himself being swept away into dark lands under strange moons; then, almost before he knew what was happening, the unadventurous Mr Baggins found that Gandalf had recommended him for the job of Burglar and he was heading off on a quest for adventure.

Which is where the map came in. Drawn on parchment, it was given to Thorin Oakenshield (together with an intricately-shaped key) by Gandalf who explained that it had been made by the dwarf's grandfather, Thror. It showed the Lonely

Mountain with Smaug (drawn in red) flying above it and another dragon wriggling its way across the paper towards 'The Desolation of Smaug', an area of tree-stumps, burnt and blackened by dragon's fire.

Thorin and his companions didn't know it at first, but the map was more than just a guide to reaching the Mountain – it also told them how to use the key to get inside. No sooner had Tolkien written this map into his story, than he decided that he should make a drawing of it.

The Hobbit was never intended for publication; Tolkien wrote it as a serial to read to his three sons on winter evenings after tea. As he did so, he took Bilbo and the others through a land of wondrous places, peopled with outlandish creatures possessing magical powers. In fact, they had scarcely left the safety of Bilbo's village, Hobbiton-across-the-Water, before they fell headlong into the threatening company of a group of idiotic, but bloodthirsty, trolls.

After this hazardous beginning, Gandalf led Bilbo and the dwarves by a perilous route, slithering and slipping down a zig-zag path, to the peaceful valley of Rivendell and then, across a narrow bridge over a tumbling river, to the Last Homely

House. It was in Rivendell, on midsummer's eve, that Elrond, the master of that house, discovered a wonderful secret. Thror's map carried moon-letters – runes, that could be read only when the map was held up to the white light of a moon of the same shape and season as that of the day on which they were written. Raising the ancient map to the moon's broad silver crescent, Elrond was able to read the runes and reveal their hidden message. . .

Eventually, the travellers left Rivendell and began their adventures in earnest, journeying over hill and under hill, through a world that seems as real as the one around us – but, of course, more magical. The geography of that world had its own excitements: there were high, windy mountain passes where lightning split the darkness and huge stone-giants hurled great rocks at one another; there was a tangled maze of airless passageways under the mountains where ugly, wicked goblins lurked; and, way down, in darkest darkness, a lake of icy coldness where, on a slimy island of rock, lived Gollum – a treacherous, pale-eyed, hissing creature who made a horrible swallowing noise in his throat. It was here, in this dank, subterranean labyrinth, that Bilbo chanced upon a magic ring that gave the wearer the power of invisibility.

Gollum was just one of the many strange, fabulous and terrifying beings that hindered (and, occasionally, helped) Bilbo and the dwarves during their journey beyond the Edge of the Wild. There was the Great Goblin, huge-headed and bad-hearted; there were evil wolves, or Wargs, with blazing eyes and gnashing teeth; and there was the Lord of the Eagles who, with his brothers, came down from the sky like a huge shadow to help the company at a moment of desperate danger. There was also Beorn, the skin-changer – sometimes a great black bear, sometimes a great, strong, black-haired and bearded man – who welcomed the travellers into his house where the air was full of the buzzing and whirring of bees and where they were waited upon by beautiful white ponies, long-bodied grey dogs and a large coal-black ram.

Less hospitable – especially after the cobwebbed terrors of Mirkwood, with its loathsome army of pop-eyed, hairy-legged spiders – was the hall of the Elvenking who, wearing a crown of berries and red leaves, condemned the dwarves to be held prisoner in his dungeon for having trespassed in his realm.

Beyond mountain and forest, they came first to Esgaroth (or Lake-town), the great wooden city built upon the Long Lake, and then to the dark and silent Lonely Mountain. On the mountain's western slopes, guided by Thror's map and the message of its moon-letters, Bilbo and the dwarves found a secret door and a long, hot, smoky tunnel down into the lair of Smaug, the vast red-golden dragon who, with folded wings and huge coiled tail, lay upon a great mound of gold and gems and jewels.

Bilbo had a riddling conversation with Smaug – whom he addressed as the Chiefest and Greatest of Calamities – but, on discovering that there were intruders inside the Lonely Mountain and that they had received help from the Lake-men, the dragon became very angry and flew off to attack the town of Esgaroth. Shortly after reaching what is one of the most exciting parts of the story, Tolkien stopped writing; and, although he improvised an ending to the tale for his children, nothing more of *The Hobbit* was put down on paper.

Incomplete though it was, Tolkien showed the story – and the drawing of Thror's map – to some of his friends in Oxford, one of whom mentioned it to a representative from the publishing firm of George Allen & Unwin. As a result, the typescript was borrowed and read, and Tolkien was soon being encouraged to finish the tale so that it might be considered for publication.

Tolkien set to work again, writing about the bitter arguments which the dwarves had with the Lake-men of Esgaroth and the elves of Mirkwood over the dragon's treasure. Then he swiftly brought the story to a breathtakingly exciting climax in which a vast army of marauding goblins, wolves and Wargs attacked the Lonely Mountain and dwarves, men and elves were forced to unite against a common enemy in a terrible conflict that came to be known as the Battle of Five Armies.

At long last, in October 1936, the completed typescript was delivered. Stanley Unwin, chairman of the publishing company, asked his young son, Rayner, to read the book and write a report on it; this he did, ending with the opinion: 'This book, with the help of maps, does not need any illustrations it is good and should appeal to all children between the ages of 5 and 9'. Master Unwin – who was ten! – was paid one shilling (the equivalent of five pence) for his views on a book that has since become a world-wide best-seller!

Rayner Unwin may have been happy to make do without illustrations, but his father decided to ask the author to draw and paint some pictures for the book. Tolkien also designed a wrapper which he decorated with runes. *The Hobbit, or There and Back Again* was published in 1937.

There were also the maps. One, drawn in black and red, showing Wilderland and the places where Bilbo's adventures happened, was designed as an end-paper for the book and John Howe has now recreated it in full colour.

The other was a copy of Thror's map, which the author wanted to have printed in the first chapter of the book, at the point at which Gandalf shows the map to Bilbo and the dwarves. Smaug, the inscription (signed with the runes representing the initials of Thror and his son, Thrain) and the secret door (marked with the rune for 'D') ᛞ were printed in red.

These runes – which had caught the imagination of Bilbo who 'loved maps' and 'liked runes and letters and cunning handwriting' – were, in Tolkien's words, 'old letters originally

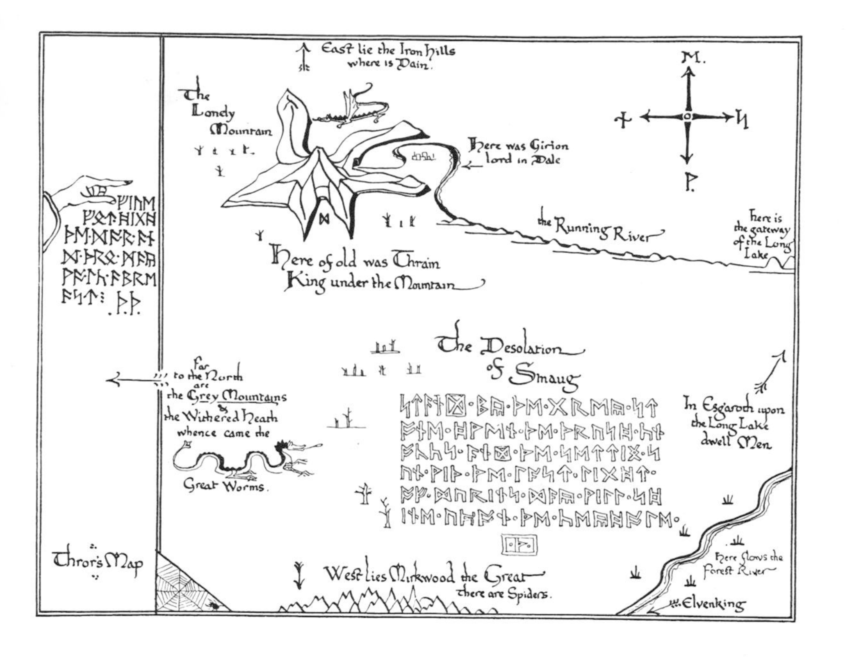

used for cutting or scratching on wood, stone, or metal, and so were thin and angular'. Some years after the publication of *The Hobbit*, he wrote to a friend giving a key which could be used to read the runes. You will find Tolkien's letter (and a translation) on the next page.

As for the secret moon-letters, Tolkien had asked for them to be printed using 'invisible lettering', but the publishers thought this too expensive and, eventually, the map (with the moon-letters completely visible) appeared as the front end-paper to the book.

At the end of *The Hobbit*, Gandalf tells Bilbo: 'You are a very fine person, Mr Baggins, and I am very fond of you; but you are only quite a little fellow in a wide world. . . ' However, when J. R. R. Tolkien had first written the line: 'In a hole in the ground there lived a hobbit,' he had not realized quite how

PROFESSOR TOLKIEN
MERTON COLLEGE
OXFORD

3. MANOR ROAD
OXFORD
Telephone: 47108

*TH*RE MANOR ROAD
SUNDAY NOV[E]MBER
*THE TH*IRTIE*TH*

D*E*AR MRS FARRER: OF COURSE I WILL SIGN YO
UR COPY OF *TH*E HOBBIT. I AM HONOURED BY *TH*E
RECWEST. IT IS GOOD NEWS *TH*AT *TH*E BOOK IS OBTAIN
ABLE AGAIN. *TH*E NEXT BOOK WILL CO[N]TAIN MORE D
ETAILED INFORMATION ABOUT RUNES AND O*TH*ER
ALFABETS IN RESPO[N]SE TO MANY ENCWIRIES. IN
*TH*E M*E*ANTIME WHILE *TH*E GR*E*AT WORK IS BEI*NG* FINIS[H]
ED I WONDER IF YOU WOULD LIKE A PROPER
KEY TO THE SPECIAL DWARVIS[H] ADAPTATION
OF *TH*E E*NG*LIS[H] RUNIC ALFABET ONLY PART OF
WHICH A*PP*EARS IN *TH*E HO*BB*IT INCLUDI*NG TH*E COVER.
WE ENIOYED LAST MONDAY EUENI*NG* VERY MU
CH AND HOPE FOR A RETURN MATCH SOON.
YOURS SINCERELY
J. R. R. TOLKIEN

wide a world it was. Although the only name that is given to the land where Bilbo's adventures take place is Wilderland, it is part of Middle-earth, an imaginary world which Tolkien had begun to create in 1917.

The earliest myths and legends of the First Age of Middle-earth were chronicled in a work which eventually became known as *The Silmarillion*; and, as Tolkien told *The Hobbit* to his sons, he began drawing on the mythology and history of Middle-earth, until it eventually became clear that this was, as he put it, 'the world into which Mr Baggins strayed'. However, Bilbo's escapades in Middle-earth turned out to be only a prologue to a more ambitious story. . .

The book was so successful that Tolkien's publishers were soon asking for 'another book about the Hobbit' and, three months after the publication of *The Hobbit*, he began to write just such a book. Where *The Hobbit* had begun with a chapter called 'An Unexpected Party', the new book was to open with a chapter entitled 'A Long-Expected Party', in which Bilbo used his magic ring to disappear at his own eleventy-first birthday party.

The ring proved to be far more powerful that anyone might have guessed from reading *The Hobbit*: it was one of several rings of great power forged by the Dark Lord Sauron (who had been referred to in *The Hobbit* as 'the Necromancer') in order to control the people of Middle-earth – elves, dwarves and mortal men. This ring, however, was the One Ring that controlled all the others.

When Bilbo left the Shire, the ring passed to his nephew, Frodo Baggins, who was caught up in another perilous adventure, this time journeying south to the shadow-filled Land of Mordor, in order to destroy the ring and Sauron's power.

It was to take J. R. R. Tolkien twelve years to write that story which he called *The Lord of the Rings* and which was published in three volumes: *The Fellowship of the Ring* and *The Two Towers* in 1954 and *The Return of the King* in 1955. As with *The Hobbit*, maps were an important part of telling the story and since, as Tolkien said, it is impossible to make a map of a story after it has been written, he made (and adapted) them as he went along. One of these maps, re-drawn by John Howe, is available as *The Map of Tolkien's Middle-earth* in a companion edition to this map. With them, it is possible to follow the journeys of Bilbo and Frodo Baggins – there and back again.

PLACES ON THE MAP OF WILDERLAND

BEORN'S HOUSE, surrounded by a high thorn-hedge and approached through a broad wooden gate, was a cluster of low wooden, thatched buildings – a house, barns, stables, sheds and row upon row of straw bee-hives. This was the home of Beorn, a giant of a man with a thick black beard and hair, great bare arms and legs with knotted muscles, who could change his shape into that of a bear. In Beorn's hall – lit by beeswax candles and with a fireplace in the middle – the travellers were entertained, the food and drink being served by Beorn's animal attendants.

CARROCK, a great rock – 'almost a hill of stone, like a last outpost of the distant mountains' – named by Beorn, the shape-changer who called it '*the* Carrock' because it was the only one near his home and he knew it well; indeed, he had cut steps into its steep side and Gandalf remembered having seen Beorn sitting there one night watching the moon sinking towards the MISTY MOUNTAINS and growling in the tongue of bears.

DESOLATION OF SMAUG, the land around the LONELY MOUNTAIN. Laid waste by the dragon, Smaug, it had little grass and no bushes nor trees other than broken and blackened stumps.

ELF-PATH, the way through MIRKWOOD taken by Bilbo and his companions. The path was narrow and wound in and out among the tree trunks and was crossed by the ENCHANTED RIVER. 'Don't stray off the track!' warned Gandalf, 'if you do, it is a thousand to one you will never find it again and never get out of Mirkwood. . . '

ELVENKING'S HALLS, behind huge doors of stone, comprised a great cave (within the edge of MIRKWOOD) from which countless smaller ones opened out on every side leading, far underground, to winding passages and wide halls. It was here that the Elvenking imprisoned the dwarves in his dungeon and from which, with Bilbo's help, they escaped by barrel down the FOREST RIVER.

ENCHANTED RIVER, black and strong, flowed through the gloom of MIRKWOOD. Beorn warned Bilbo and his companions against drinking or bathing in the stream since it carried an enchantment and 'a great drowsiness and forgetfulness'. Despite this warning, one of the dwarves, Bombur, fell into the river and under its spell.

ESGAROTH (See LAKE-TOWN)

EYRIE, the Great Shelf high on the eastern slopes of the MISTY MOUNTAINS to which the Lord of the Eagles and his brothers carried the travellers after having rescued them from goblins and Wargs.

FORD, where after their escapade with the trolls, the travellers crossed the river (named in *The Lord of the Rings* as the Bruinen, or Loudwater) and so came to 'the very edge of the Wild'. It was from here that Gandalf led them along a path marked by white stones to the valley of RIVENDELL.

FOREST-GATE, an arch made by two great trees – old, strangled with ivy and hung with lichen – that, leaning together, formed the entrance to MIRKWOOD. Beyond lay a gloomy tunnel where the ELF-PATH wound away into the dark stillness of the forest.

FOREST RIVER, running south-east from the GREY MOUNTAINS, through the northern part of MIRKWOOD, past the ELVENKING'S HALLS and into the LONG LAKE. It was down this river to LAKE-TOWN that the dwarves travelled, hidden inside barrels, and so escaped from their imprisonment in the dungeon of the Elvenking.

GOBLIN GATE, the 'back-door' to the goblin kingdom on the east side of the MISTY MOUNTAINS. It had been built both as an escape route (if needed) and as a way out into the lands beyond the mountain-range, where the goblins sometimes journeyed in order to plunder, murder and enslave.

GREAT RIVER OF WILDERLAND, flowing south from the GREY MOUNTAINS and named Anduin in *The Lord of the Rings*, where the story of the river's importance in the history of Middle-earth is fully told. It was in the waters of the Great River that the One Ring, which had been cut from the hand of Sauron and was now worn by Isildur, slipped from the wearer's finger and was lost. It was later found by a hobbit-like creature called Déagol who was murdered by his friend, Sméagol, who wanted the ring for himself. Calling it his 'precious', Sméagol took the ring and went to live among the dark passageways under the MISTY MOUNTAINS. It was there that Sméagol, then known by the name 'Gollum', lost the magic ring once more and encountered Mr Bilbo Baggins, who had accidentally found it.

THE GREY MOUNTAINS of the north were never visited by Bilbo and the dwarves, but Gandalf warned them against travelling in that direction, saying that their slopes were 'simply stiff with goblins, hobgoblins, and orcs of the worst description'.

LAKE-TOWN (ESGAROTH), a town of many buildings, with wooden quays from which steps and ladders went down to the surface of the lake, built upon tall piles driven into the bed of the LONG LAKE. It was here that Bilbo and the dwarves came after their escape from the dungeon of the Elvenking. Later, Lake-town was attacked by Smaug the dragon and was set ablaze by the terrible flames of his breath. However, a single arrow, fired by Bard the Bowman, brought Smaug crashing down in ruin upon the burning town.

LONELY MOUNTAIN (or Erebor, as it is named on the maps of Middle-earth) was discovered by the ancient dwarf lord, Thrain the Old. It became the home of Thror and his family when they were driven out of the far north. Here Thror became King under the Mountain and, living in peace with the men who dwelt along the banks of the RIVER RUNNING, the dwarves added to their considerable fortune with gold and gems discovered under the mountain. The dwarves worked as smiths, making objects of great beauty and wonderful playthings for the nearby town of Dale where the toy market became the wonder of the north.

It was Thror's great wealth that brought the greedy, strong and wicked dragon, Smaug, down from the north. Those dwarves who did not escape were destroyed by Smaug, who crawled in through the Front Gate and made his lair among the treasure-filled halls beneath the mountain. Occasionally, the dragon emerged and terrorized the town of Dale, from whose people, years later, would come the dragon-slayer, Bard the Bowman. It was before this same Gate that the dwarves, the elves of MIRKWOOD and the men of LAKE-TOWN fought the Battle of Five Armies against the goblins and Wargs of the north.

but on the map of Middle-earth) stood Dol Guldur, at one time the fortress of the Necromancer (later known as the Lord of the Rings) in whose dungeon Thorin Oakenshield's father, Thrain, was held prisoner.

THE MISTY MOUNTAINS, a great mountain range running north to south in Middle-earth. Setting out from RIVENDELL Gandalf, Bilbo and the dwarves attempted to cross the mountains but were prevented by bad weather. They sheltered from the storm in a cave which proved to be a secret entrance to the goblin kingdom beneath the mountains. Bilbo and the dwarves were seized by goblin soldiers, but Gandalf, who had remained free, attacked the goblins with magic fire and killed the Great Goblin with his sword. In the struggle that followed, Bilbo was separated from his friends and, wandering lost through the maze of passageways, came to a dark lake. Here Bilbo encountered Gollum and accidentally found the slimy creature's 'precious', the magic ring that could make the wearer invisible.

It was in the Mines of Moria beneath the southern arm of these mountains (not shown on this map) that the dwarf Thorin Oakenshield's grandfather Thror was killed by Azog the Goblin and where, many years later, Bilbo's nephew and his companions were to have desperate adventures recounted in *The Lord of the Rings*.

MOUNT GUNDABAD, the goblin capital in the north where, on learning that Smaug the dragon had been killed and that the dwarves had returned to the LONELY MOUNTAIN, a vast army gathered by many secret ways in order to sweep down, storm the mountain and seize the dwarves' treasure.

OLD FORD, across the GREAT RIVER, fifty miles south of the CARROCK.

RIVENDELL, a hidden valley beyond the Edge of the Wild where the scent of trees was in the air and where a narrow bridge led to the Last Homely House. It was at Rivendell that

LONG LAKE, on which that the Lake-men had built the LAKE-TOWN, Esgaroth.

MIRKWOOD, a dense forest between the GREAT RIVER and the LONELY MOUNTAIN, described by Bilbo as having 'a sort of watching and waiting feeling'. Entering by the FOREST-GATE, the travellers followed the ELF-PATH through the still, dark and stuffy wood with its tall trees, between which great spiders had stretched cobwebs made of thick, sticky threads.

In was in this wood that they crossed the ENCHANTED RIVER, saw the Wood-elves feasting among the trees to the sound of song and harp, were attacked by an army of huge, ugly spiders and were eventually arrested and led off to the ELVENKING'S HALLS.

On the southern edge of Mirkwood (not shown on this map,